Today is a busy day
for Little Bunny.

The sun is shining, the sky is blue,
and Little Bunny has a big basket
to fill for friends like you!

Where is Little Bunny?

Little Bunny is finding flowers
to put in the basket.

Where is Little Bunny?

5¢
Cotton Candy

2¢

Little Bunny is choosing sweet treats.

Where is Little Bunny?

Little Bunny is gathering
eggs to color.

Where is Little Bunny?

Little Bunny is painting
pretty patterns on the eggs.

Where is Little Bunny?

Little Bunny is looking
for the speckled egg.
Do you see it?

Where is Little Bunny?

Little Bunny is counting
the baby chicks!

Little Bunny is hiding in the basket, ready to give you a big

surprise!

Ready for some more fun?
Cuddle up with your child and turn back
through the story to enjoy these
Look and Find activities:

Basket begins with the letter **B**.
Can you find these things
that also start with **B**?

bow

bird

bumblebee

bunny

balloon

Hop back to Little Bunny's
garden and count
these beautiful blooms:

1 red
flower

2 yellow
flowers

3 blue
flowers

4 orange flowers   **5** purple flowers

Don't these treats look delicious?
Can you find them in Little Bunny's sweet shop?

Cluck, cluck! Do you see these chickens in Little Bunny's farmyard?

Little Bunny loves to paint!
See if you can spot these shapes on the eggs:

   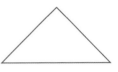

circle   square   star   triangle   heart

Little Bunny's animal friends are looking for the speckled egg, too.
Can you match each animal's name to its picture?

lamb   **squirrel**   frog   duck   fox

Can you help Little Bunny count the chicks?
How many do you see?

7, 8, 9, or 10?

Little Bunny's basket is bursting with festive fun!
Can you spot these colors in the scene?

RED   YELLOW
GREEN   BLUE
PURPLE

Follow that egg!

Use your finger to trace a path
from Little Bunny to the egg.

Start